The Adventures of Sharpie Kitten

The Adventures of Sharpie Kitten

by Rob Lewenstein

CINCINNATI BOOK PUBLISHING

The Adventures of Sharpie Kitten
by Rob Lewenstein

Published by Cincinnati Book Publishing
www.CincyBooks.com
Anthony W. Brunsman, president
Sue Ann Painter, executive editor
Michelle Kallmeyer, assistant editor
Kayla Stellwagen, designer
Allen Lute, illustrator

ISBN: 978-1-7378038-9-8
Library of Congress Control Number: 2022950480

Printed in the United States of America

First Edition, 2023

For Sabina Scribner, childhood angel
Finale Ligure, Italy
1963

Special Thanks
Nina, Meghan, Bryn, Rosie, Ben, Jeremy, Allen (for the great illustrations), Thom (for his help with the pictures), and Vicky (for all her help).

Many thanks to all!

Introduction

The Adventures of Sharpie Kitten is a magical and ongoing story about Sharpie Kitten and his animal family.

Sharpie Kitten is a large, beautiful black cat with emerald green eyes. He is animated, extremely intelligent, and very funny. He has a "cat vocabulary" of eighty-five different meows, and has the quickness of a cobra. He has an appetite of a voracious nature, though he is sleek and sports no body fat. He lives on a beautiful animal sanctuary farm in the Midwest that has crop fields and is totally surrounded by a forest of oak, maple, hickory, locust, pine, and spruce trees. The farm has sections of jungle type landscape with very thick green undergrowth, where Sharpie Kitten and his family all love to venture.

Sharpie Kitten's pals who live with him are Marja, a gorgeous gray cat with green golden eyes. She is a funny character and a devoted follower of Sharpie Kitten. The family dog is Chays. She is a very sweet Beagle who not only is a bone lover but is constantly on alert to bark and let Sharpie Kitten know if anything is going on that needs his attention. Many wild animals live on the farm, including rabbits, deer, raccoons, opossums, and many kinds of birds. And last but definitely not least, there is Leo, the baby deer.

The Adventures of Sharpie Kitten starts with the day that Sharpie Kitten was found in the Wal-Mart parking lot, and how he adapted to his environment, and how his life has progressed to this point in time. It is a wonderful story of how animals love and play and teach and learn from each other and all their sometimes hilarious and animated actions. I hope you enjoy visiting the farm and spending time with Sharpie Kitten and his animal family.

Chapter 1

Finding Sharpie Kitten

Ah, blessed sleep. It is so nice to sleep and dream. I lay here wondering why I am thinking about being asleep when I am actually awake. The reasoning comes to me quickly; my giant, black cat Purcotti is standing on my chest, kneading his claws in my skin, making sure that I am awake! It is 6:42 AM, and he and his cohort want their breakfast. Purcotti is anthracite black in color with beautiful emerald green eyes. He really resembles a small panther! "Bruuuup," he meows ("Get up!"). I pet him and tell him, "Ok, Purcotti, I'm getting up."

I throw on my clothes and go downstairs with Purcotti in hot pursuit. I turn on the morning news, turn on the coffee, and collect the four bowls of my animal family. The house is alive with activity. Chays the Beagle runs to the door to go out. Afja (pronounced "Af-ya"), who is a large female gray tiger cat, her sister Marja (pronounced "Mar-ya"), who is gray and brown (they both have beautiful golden-green eyes), and Purcotti start Big Time Cat Wrestling. This is an activity that they do before every meal, not just for fun and excitement, but to show the order of leadership within the family. They run crazily after each other around the kitchen table, jumping on each other with excitement and joyous energy. Afja always defeats Marja, and then she attacks Purcotti. Afja swings a right and then a left at him. He outweighs her by nine pounds, and after a very short scuffle with fur and paws in every position, he looks at her, grabs her, throws her down, jumping on top of her, holding her down. She hisses and gives up. Purcotti stands up, raises his head with his green eyes sparkling meowing, "Browww ynk ynk rrow!" (English translation: "I am King!") I grab the three cat bowls filled with their favorite dry and can cat foods and place them on the floor in their own places for their breakfast as I dodge them with my feet. I take Chays' bowl to her place, and let her in the house to eat. I only then have a chance to watch the morning news and drink a cup of coffee.

By the time the news is over, and I have drunk my coffee, all three cats are sitting on the couch around me, and Chays is at my feet, waiting to see if I will eat something that they will get to share. I have another cup of coffee while I make a list of things that I need to buy at the grocery store. I gather paper and pen; the cats leave and go to their bowls for seconds of breakfast. They eat like pigs, though they are not related to pigs! They finish eating as I finish my grocery list, and I pick up their bowls and put them up on the counter. If I leave the bowls on the floor, Chays will eat every morsel of their food as she also eats like a pig!

I shower, dress, and turn on some music for the animal family. It makes them more comfortable to have music on so that they don't feel alone while I am gone. It was Purcotti's turn to pick the music, and his choice was Johann Sebastian Bach's Second Suite in B minor.

I go outside and see what a glorious day it is. The sun is shining beautifully, making designs through the leaves of trees and undergrowth, sparkling with drops of dew. Sasha, one of the mother deer that lives on the farm, runs happily through the field by the house. She stops and looks at me while she nibbles grass, uninhibited and unafraid. I wave to her as I get in my car to leave. I start the car, drive a few feet, and then stop to let a rabbit go past our secluded gravel lane. She goes into a hayfield on the left side of the lane. I thank God for such a beautiful place to live!

I drive into town, arrive at Wal-Mart, and I park my car. I walk towards the store and with my peripheral vision I spot a moving object under a green 4x4 pick-up truck. It is a tiny black kitten! The pick-up truck just started his engine, so I ran over to the truck and just in time, I bent over and grabbed the little kitten from under the truck's back wheel!

I held up the tiny kitten and looked at him; he was a beautiful black kitten with sable red overtones in his fur with the sunlight shining on him. He looked at me and had the same gorgeous emerald, green eyes that Purcotti has. He made a tiny meow, "Yenk yenk" ("Thanks for saving me!") and started purring! I put him in the passenger seat with a partially open window so he would have plenty of air. It was not too warm out yet, so with me hurrying, I knew that he would not overheat in the car.

As I walked into the store and started shopping, I thought: "Someone dropped off the tiny kitten, and I have three cats, one dog living in our home, so what is the big deal of having another family member?" I got all the needed supplies, and I got some extra cat snacks to feed the kitten as I figured that he was probably very hungry.

When I got back to the car, the kitten stood on the steering wheel looking out the front windshield. I put the supplies in the trunk and grabbed a bag of cat snacks. I got in the car and put the kitten in the passenger seat, opened the cat snacks, and put some on the seat for him to eat. He devoured the food in twenty seconds and looked at me for more. I told him that he had enough for now, as I didn't want him to get sick on the drive home.

As I drove home, I wondered if my animal family would be happy to receive him as a new family member, or would they be mean to him? Time would soon tell. The kitten was on my lap purring loudly, standing up and laying down, not wanting to miss anything that was going on in his life. I could tell that he had an immense character just by the way he was acting.

He was animated, grabbing my shirttail and playing with it as he was having a ball.

I decided it was time to name the kitten and after watching him, he reminded me of one of my favorite hockey players, Chicago Blackhawks forward, Patrick Sharp. Patrick Sharp's nickname is Sharpie, so that is how Sharpie Kitten got his name. I said his name out loud, and Sharpie Kitten responded instantly, looking at me with those beautiful green eyes. It is funny that he was named after a hockey player, because during Sharpie's life, when hockey was on TV, he would jump on the TV stand and bat the hockey players on the screen, actually following the puck as it moved around the ice!

Chapter 2

Sharpie Kitten Meets His New Family

Sharpie Kitten and I arrived home, and I quickly brought all the groceries into the house and put everything away.

Purcotti was lying on the floor by the sofa, enjoying the sun that was shining through the window. Afja and Marja were lying together on a sofa listening to one of Marja's favorite songs, Van Morrison's "Dancing in the Moonlight." Chays was sleeping on her back by the fireplace. It looked like the perfect time to bring in Sharpie Kitten to meet his new family.

I went to the car door and out he came and he instantly jumped on a bumblebee which he swatted. Luckily for him, it flew away instead of stinging him! He ran out in the grass and dug a hole and relieved himself, covering everything up with his tiny paw throwing dirt every which way until he was convinced that all was clean.

I picked him up and walked into the house holding him in my arms, and instantly all three cats looked up and saw the kitten. I walked over to the food area and set him down on the floor while the cats walked over and stopped very close to Sharpie Kitten. They didn't move at all, just staring at him. He didn't seem to be afraid as he looked back at them, in a high kitten voice he said, "Yenk, yenk!" ("How's it going?"). Purcotti, Afja, and Marja walked right up to him looking at him and sniffing all over his body. Sharpie Kitten stood there looking back at them, not moving a muscle. Afja sniffed his ear, hissed loudly at him, running four feet away and looking at him. Marja sniffed his back, hissed and growled loudly at him moving backward as she growled. Purcotti, who was king of the home, felt that he needed to check him out thoroughly. Purcotti batted his tail back and forth, sniffing and walking around him three times, finally stopping in front of Sharpie Kitten; they were touching nose to

nose. Purcotti meowed, "Rouw rouwwww!" ("Who in the world are you?") The meow was very loud, then he too hissed at Sharpie Kitten!

I watched this transpire, and I hoped that bringing Sharpie Kitten here was not going to be a mistake, especially if he might be mistreated by his new family. I saw Chays come over to see what was going on, and she spotted the kitten and stopped a couple of feet away from him. Chays walked over to him slowly, and with Sharpie Kitten looking her in the eye, rubbed himself against her fur. Chays licked him in the face knocking him sideways. They went back to lay down by the fireplace, totally unaffected by the newcomer!

I showed Sharpie Kitten his new food bowl, and where it would be placed, and where the water bowls were. I then took him to the two litter boxes so that he would know where to use the bathroom; and I set him free to roam around and get used to his new environment on his own. All the other cats kept their distance from Sharpie Kitten, even while eating the evening meal, and after they were very stand-offish.

All the animosity and ostracizing shown by Purcotti, Afja, and Marja didn't seem to faze Sharpie Kitten. He found cat toys lying around, and he jumped on one after another playing wildly, and letting out his high-pitched meow, "Mink mink," he said! ("This is great stuff!") The other cats remained nonplussed and continued to stay away from him.

I watched the Blackhawks game, brushed my teeth, and went to bed hoping that tomorrow would be a nicer day for my animal family and their new member.

I awoke at 6:45 AM. There was no Purcotti walking on my chest, nor was Afja or Marja jumping on my legs. None of them were here. Even Chays was absent. I didn't have long to wonder or to see what was happening in the house. I then heard a loud BANG and scraping noises from downstairs. I jumped out of bed, threw on shorts and a t-shirt, and ran downstairs.

What I saw was an animal circus of the three-ring variety. Afja and

Purcotti were excitedly wrestling together on one spot. A lizard had gotten in the house and Marja was attacking it. Chays was running full speed around the dining room table. It didn't take long to see why Chays was running so fast; Sharpie Kitten was on her back with his little paws gripping her sides holding on for dear life, riding her like she was a horse! Chays made three fast trips around the table before Sharpie Kitten had other ideas. He jumped off Chays's back only to land right on top of Purcotti and Afja, instantly joining the wrestling match! Afja tried to grab Sharpie Kitten, but he jumped on her head and on Purcotti's neck. Purcotti grabbed him in his strong front legs and rolled over with Sharpie Kitten batting at his ears! This went on for another minute, and finally, as all cats will do, they stopped wrestling and stood up together to catch their breath. Sharpie Kitten stood there looking at the other three cats while they looked back at him. Purcotti, Afja, and Marja started walking around in a circle with Sharpie Kitten in the middle. Purcotti meowed, "Merrrrouw" ("You'll do") and then he walked over to the food station, waiting for breakfast. The rest of the animal family walked around my feet, while I prepared their food.

I gave them all their food and as I watched them eat, it was apparent that Sharpie Kitten had been accepted into our animal family. The confirmation of Sharpie Kitten's acceptance was affirmed after breakfast was finished.

All the animals went outside to explore and roam, and Purcotti came over to Sharpie Kitten, batted his tail, and then quickly licked his head! All was well in Purcotti's Kingdom. The interaction of the four cats became a normal daily occurrence. Sharpie Kitten not only played with all the others but he learned from them, especially from Purcotti, as he had become Sharpie Kitten's mentor.

Sharpie Kitten would hang out with Purcotti and listen to him so he could understand the animal world. Purcotti would tell him, "Brrrrup ank ank"

("You have to be smart and extremely tough, Sharpie Kitten."), and Sharpie Kitten totally believed him.

Sharpie Kitten decided that he had to begin to prove himself to his new family. He had been on the farm for about a month and a half, and on a seemingly normal day when everyone was outside roaming and playing, Afja decided to show her Alpha side to Sharpie Kitten, and she jumped on him. Sharpie Kitten loudly meowed, "Burrow rerryenk!" ("You can't hurt me Afja!"). He quickly got up and ran to the house. He jumped high on the corner of the house, grabbing the wood and climbing all the way up eighteen feet high to a ledge! Sharpie Kitten was standing on the ledge, looking down at us, and also looking at the upper deck which was ten feet away from him and close to eight feet below him. I was petrified watching this unfold in front of me. I ran over and got directly under Sharpie Kitten so if he jumped and missed his footing, I could catch him and prevent him from being injured or killed. He was walking back and forth on the ledge, looking down at us, and more importantly, looking at the deck ten feet away from him. He was at the edge of the ledge and stopped moving completely. With all four animals and myself watching, he compressed himself like a spring, and with a high pitched meow, "Reeeow" ("Here I go!"), he jumped off the ledge, flying through the air, touching his front paws on the top of the deck rail, and gliding down to the floor of the deck! He turned around toward us and with his head through the handrails, meowed in total triumph, "Annkk annkk annkk annkk" ("Great jump, ha!"). Sharpie Kitten had done no damage to himself at all, and he had earned the respect of his animal family in the process of his climb and jump.

The animal family continued their normal routine of playing and wrestling happily in complete harmony, vigor, and joy as time moved forward on the farm.

Chapter 3

Fun Times and Educating Sharpie Kitten

Happy months had gone by since Sharpie Kitten's arrival on the farm, and there was much amusement among the animal family.

Afja, who is a very funny character, has a devilish sense of humor to go along with it. She is the number two Alpha animal behind Purcotti in the family, so she decided that she was going to exert her power over as many of the animal family as she could. Chays was lying on a sofa and she was dreaming of chasing rabbits, with her paws moving back and forth quickly, along with making muted dream barks. Afja spied her lying there, and she couldn't possibly let an opportunity like this go to waste without messing with Chays. Afja jumped silently and with stealth onto the back of the sofa right above where Chays was lying, looking the situation over and formulating her plan of attack. Purcotti, Marja, and Sharpie Kitten were all waiting and watching from their vantage points around the living room. Afja knew that she was in the spotlight which she loved. She emulated an Olympic diver, arched her back, leaned far over and raised her left paw high in the air. After a few seconds of waiting, she struck Chays right on her nose! Chays awakened from her wonderful dream, yipped loudly, jumping up and trying to figure out what had hit her. It didn't take her long to figure it out, as Afja was sitting above her on top of the sofa with her devilish cat grin of satisfaction! Chays growled at Afja but she was intimidated by her attack; and she jumped off the sofa, went across the room, and lay down by the cool stones of the large fireplace to get some peace. Even though Afja regularly played tricks on Chays and Sharpie Kitten rode on her back as she ran around the table a few times a week, she took it all in good humor. Chays is a good-natured and very happy Beagle!

After most play, Purcotti and Sharpie Kitten would go up to the attic and have psychological and philosophical conversations about life. Sharpie Kitten was growing like a weed, and Purcotti realized that Sharpie Kitten was capable of doing great things, as he had already done things that the rest of the family had never done. Purcotti also realized that besides Sharpie Kitten's incredible brilliance and abilities, he was still uneducated, so he took it upon himself to teach him everything he knew. He wanted Sharpie Kitten to understand and be ready for anything that life could bring him in the future.

Purcotti talked to Sharpie Kitten about dangerous situations that could occur. He told him about the life threatening dangers of cars and trucks hitting animals when they went into the road without looking. Unsuspecting animals could be hurt badly or killed, and that scared Sharpie Kitten while he listened! He told him about people who would shoot at animals with guns for no apparent reason, hurting or killing them. He talked about snakes, and how dangerous rattlesnakes and copperheads could be to animals if they were bitten by them. He showed Sharpie Kitten "The Official Snake Guide of the Midwest," showing him the snakes that were not poisonous and the snakes that were poisonous and that the rattlesnake could be deadly. He talked to Sharpie Kitten for many days, hours at a time, teaching him about everything he could think of that was important to animals. He spoke to him about hunting animals like rabbits, chipmunks, and birds. Although it is very sad that animals are predators, we humans have to endure animals' predatory actions as well as our own!

Purcotti educated Sharpie Kitten about the importance of music in his life. Purcotti's favorite band of all time was Brian Setzer's great band, "Stray Cats," and he would play that band's songs for Sharpie Kitten. The two black cats, one huge, and one still small were becoming very close and had deep love for each other.

During this period when Sharpie Kitten was being mentored by Purcotti, he was also learning tricks from Afja and Marja. He was a sponge for information and learning, and he realized something special; he was different from the other members of his animal family. Sharpie Kitten was getting stronger and physically and mentally he could assimilate thoughts and ideas which he easily implemented. He would go outside and challenge the other animals to games of skill and intelligence. He challenged Mino the grasshopper to a jumping contest while using a physics formula (he had gone on the computer for the first time) that explained how to use the maximum speed and torque from his back legs. It taught him how to jump higher and further with each jump. Mino and Sharpie Kitten started jumping at the line that they had drawn in the grass, and after three jumps, Mino conceded defeat, as he had been beaten at the thing he did best: jumping!

A young deer named Johann came out of the woods to visit the animal family frequently during that summer. He was always boasting about how well he could jump, how agile he was, and how fast he could run. All of the animal family always listened to him. Still they were getting tired of his boasting his own virtues to everyone. Sharpie Kitten, who always analyzed what he saw and heard, had figured out the perfect way to bring Johann back down to earth. He called Johann over and talked to him about running. Johann told him that he was the fastest young deer on the farm, as he had beaten all the other young deer that he had raced. Sharpie Kitten looked him in his beautiful brown eyes, and told him, "Braa ruk ruk murrup!" ("Johann, I challenge you to a race!"). Johann looked at Sharpie Kitten, and with his deer laugh ("Bleeehaa"), accepted Sharpie Kitten's challenge. Sharpie Kitten had watched Johann run a couple of times. He realized that in a straight line, Johann could beat him easily, so after much thought, Sharpie Kitten laid out a perfect racecourse, designed especially for himself! He made the course thirty yards long in a narrow oval shape, which gave the course very sharp curves at each end.

At eight-thirty the next morning, Johann came out of the woods with his mom, Doerniece, and his twin sister, Jeni, who wanted to watch Johann win his race. Sharpie Kitten showed Johann the racetrack, and Johann said, "Blehh, blehhh" ("He was ready to race."). Purcotti, who was amused, walked over to explain the race rules, as he was the race master. The race would consist of two trips around the thirty-yard course. Purcotti got Johann and Sharpie Kitten on the starting line, and said, "Mraawah, marrrwah, mrrp!" ("On your mark, get set, GO!"). They both took off with Johann in the early lead. They came quickly to the first turn, Johann was running so fast that he had to go an extra five yards to slow down enough to turn and get back on the racecourse. Sharpie Kitten knew this would happen because he was so much closer to the ground than Johann. He could turn on a dime, while Johann having long legs had to give himself room to turn. At the first turn, Sharpie Kitten took the lead. He was flying down the backstretch about to turn on the second lap as Johann nearly caught up to him on that straight. Sharpie Kitten took the next curves to start the second lap with ease, flying up the next straight stretch while Johann again had to run way past the curve to get himself turned for lap number two. Sharpie Kitten's formula of torque, handling stability, and inertia became evident as he ran with ease and watched Johann with his peripheral vision, falling further and further back with each passing curve. By the end of the race, Sharpie Kitten had a ten-yard lead, and finished the race with vigor.

Johann was completely surprised that he didn't win the race and his face showed the sadness of losing. His sister Jeni brought him a grape leaf to eat for conciliation. Sharpie Kitten came over to Johann and in good sportsmanship, offered his paw. Johann accepted Sharpie Kitten's paw and offered up his right hoof. They shook paw and hoof together. Sharpie Kitten said to Johann, "Burr upp rupprow!" ("Nice race Johann!"). Sharpie Kitten watched smiling as Johann and his family walked away into woods; Sharpie Kitten was really happy!

After all the high calorie activity of the race, Sharpie Kitten was starving! I always have to pick the cats' bowls off the floor and put them on the counter covered, because if I don't pick them up, Chays will sneak up looking side to side, making sure she is unobserved, and wolf down any cat food that is left in their bowls! Sharpie Kitten had been watching me feed his animal family along with himself for quite some time and he realized something interesting. He could circumvent me having to put down the cat bowls to eat if he wanted to do that. He walked over to the refrigerator and pushed his nose into the seal of the door and exerted pressure. The door began to open and he stuck his left paw into the edge of the door, swinging it open. His beautiful green eyes were sparkling as he reached up in the refrigerator with his paw and threw an open can of cat food out onto the floor! The can rolled around on the floor and landed upside down. That didn't deter Sharpie Kitten in the least. He grabbed the can with both paws picking it up, dislodged the plastic lid with his chin and dumped all the food on the floor! Purcotti, Afja, and Marja were watching him carefully to see what he was up to, and when the cat food hit the floor, they all ran over to the unexpected Shangri-La and joined him in the feast!

Sharpie Kitten continued to play and wrestle and test his strength. He regularly defeated Marja, who being a beta cat and not as aggressive as the other family members, didn't mind losing. Marja, on the other hand, though not nearly as strong as Purcotti, was still winning about half the time that she and Sharpie Kitten wrestled. Purcotti, who was king and very powerful, always beat Sharpie Kitten, but he never gave up and was giving Purcotti more and more of a battle as he grew bigger and stronger with time. Sharpie Kitten was using different tactics every time he would wrestle, and he had come up with his favorite hold to date. It was his claw hold! He didn't always win, and had never won so far against Purcotti, but he had earned the respect of his animal family members. And please don't forget about Chays; Sharpie

Kitten regularly would try to get her to wrestle and at least once a week, Sharpie Kitten jumped on her back and rode her around the table with Chays running as fast as she could run to try and throw Sharpie Kitten off her back. Chays' tactic never worked, and Sharpie Kitten rode her until he decided to jump off of her, with a look of satisfaction on his face!

Mid-autumn had come to the farm with the last of the beautiful leaves turning from red and gold to brown, and dropping off the tree branches. It was raining hard on this particular Tuesday morning, and the drops glistened on the grass and trees, and bounced off the deck and steps. All of the animal family was manning the windows looking out at the rain. They didn't like getting wet but they still wanted to be co-joined with the outdoors. The family, bored of watching the nonstop rain and all, decided to take naps; that is except for Sharpie Kitten. He was vigilant in his window and continued to watch the rain, waiting for it to stop so that he could go outside. Sharpie Kitten loved walking around the farm, taking in its splendor and beauty, and to contemplate the ideas and thoughts that he had learned from Purcotti in their mentoring sessions. The rain had finally slowed down to a sprinkle and Sharpie Kitten decided that he had waited to go outside long enough.

He went down to the basement and out the dog door to the outside world. The trees were dripping large drops of water, and the grass, weeds and underbrush were totally drenched. He walked around the house and entered into Purcotti's Jungle. He watched the birds sitting on tree limbs, and in one of the huge oak tree branches, two mated squirrels were jumping around from branch to branch. They were carrying fallen walnuts to their den for food in the cold winter months that were ahead.

Sharpie Kitten had walked to the western edge of Purcotti's Jungle and was startled at a loud crash in the bushes. Sharpie Kitten jumped in the air and turned around to see what had made the loud noise; a small brown bear had walked into the yard! The bear and Sharpie Kitten had instantly spotted each other at the exact same time. Sharpie Kitten was thinking of Purcotti's training, wasting not a second, he went into action. He ran over to a big red Oak tree and quickly climbed up to the first branch and turned to look down at the bear. At this point in Sharpie Kitten's life, he didn't realize that a bear could also climb trees, and when the bear started to climb the tree after him, he did the only thing that he could do, and that was to keep climbing to stay ahead of the bear. The next limb that Sharpie Kitten came to was about twenty feet off the ground, and when he looked down, the bear was still in hot pursuit. He climbed up to the third limb which was about thirty feet off the ground. The limbs were getting smaller as Sharpie Kitten climbed higher and higher in the tree. He realized that the bear would have trouble with the climb as the limbs grew smaller because of his great weight, but as he looked down the bear was still climbing after him.

The bear had climbed so fast that Sharpie Kitten was forced to go out on the limb away from the trunk to stay out of the bear's reach. The limb got smaller and smaller the further Sharpie Kitten got from the tree trunk. The bear was still coming after him, though the bear was having trouble with the small limbs. The limb was bending greatly from the weight of the two animals, and the bear got scared that he would fall, so he retreated back to the trunk of the tree. Sharpie Kitten saw the bear retreat, but he knew that his position was tenuous at best. He was nearly out to the end of the limb, and he knew that the bear would wait him out until he gave up and came back toward the trunk, and then Sharpie Kitten would be dinner for the bear! Sharpie Kitten's superior intelligence came to the forefront, and he started looking around for another way to escape the angry bear.

There was a large Spruce Tree about fifteen feet away from the Oak tree in which the two combatants were temporarily planted. Sharpie Kitten made

up his mind quickly; he was going to jump from the Oak tree, fifteen feet through the air and down about eight feet to where a secure limb was located in the large Spruce tree. Sharpie Kitten knew that he needed some momentum and speed to be able to jump the distance needed to reach the Spruce tree, so he carefully moved backwards on the very wet and slick limb, back towards the bear. The bear was watching Sharpie Kitten and he thought to himself, "Now I've got him, he's coming back!" Sharpie Kitten moved back about six feet, and was about eight feet away from the bear. He leaped forward as fast and as safely as he could go, and getting close to the end of the limb, leaped high in the air, flying towards the Spruce tree! Sharpie Kitten was lucky that he was fast, as he barely made the big Spruce limb, grabbing on for dear life with his claws as he landed sideways on the limb! He let out a "Meeeerowww!" ("Thank God I'm safe!").

Sharpie Kitten turned and looked at the bear, and realized that he wasn't exactly safe, at least not yet. The tenacious bear had begun to walk out the limb to see if he could continue to follow Sharpie Kitten, but to his consternation, the limb would not support his weight. The bear was sitting there looking at Sharpie Kitten, and Sharpie Kitten was staring back at the bear. Sharpie Kitten looked around and saw from his studies that there were weapons at hand that he could use if he was strong enough to use them. There were big soaking wet Spruce cones hanging all around him, and Sharpie Kitten was going to attack the bear with them!

He pulled back the limb with his front claws grabbing deeply in the wood exactly where a Spruce cone hung. He kept pulling back until the limb was really bent and what he had made was an ancient catapult, like the Trojans and Greeks used centuries ago in their wars. He lined up the bear in his sights who was watching unsuspecting of any attack upon him. Sharpie Kitten let the limb fly violently forward, shooting the Spruce cone from the tree and it struck the bear right in the nose! The bear roared from the surprise and from the sting of the cone hitting him. Sharpie Kitten didn't wait for anything and he went to the closest Spruce cone, and before the bear could move, unleashed his next attack. The second cone struck the bear in his left ear! The angry stinging bear decided that he was going down the tree away from those horrible cones. Sharpie Kitten had gotten to the next cone and was preparing to shoot it as soon as he could, but the bear was smart too. He climbed down the back side of the Oak tree away from any projectiles that could be fired at him. He had decided that when he got to the ground, he would climb the Spruce tree and get Sharpie Kitten once and for all, but as soon as he touched the ground, Sharpie Kitten fired his next cone with precise accuracy, striking him under his right eye! The bear again roared his pain and displeasure. Sharpie had jumped down a couple of limbs and he was closer to the ground, and he let fly his next cone. He struck the bear in the stomach, and the bear turned and ran about twenty feet away, turning to look at Sharpie Kitten. Sharpie Kitten got the next cone and fired hitting the bear in his lip. That was it and the bear gave up and turned to run just as Sharpie kitten fired his last cone striking the bear on his behind making him jump, roar, and run simultaneously!

Sharpie Kitten had defeated the bear who was ten times his size and had superior strength, but there was one thing that Sharpie Kitten proved, that intelligence will win battles most of the time. But there was one more thing that Sharpie Kitten realized and that was that he had SUPER POWERS!

Sharpie Kitten climbed down from the Spruce tree and walked to the house and scratched on the door. I let him in and I saw that he was soaking wet. I got a towel and dried him off, and he jumped up on the sofa rolling around with a smile on his face.

Chapter 4

Things Change on the Farm

It was deep into autumn on the farm, and the very last of any green leaves on the Willow was the only color left, beside the Pines, Spruce, and Cedar trees. There was a bush or two that stayed green, but the brilliance of warm weather green was totally gone for the year. One could still walk by the evergreens and have the wonderful smells and see the birds coming to the feeders hanging by the house, but it was evident that winter and cold temperatures were going to be here soon. Mother deer were already coming to the feeding station by the garden to eat corn that I put out for them twice a day. I always wonder what deer can find to eat when it is cold with ice and snow? I am happy that the corn helps them to survive winter months.

All of the animal family were happy and playful until one morning something was amiss. I got up in the morning to feed everyone and start the day, and I saw that Purcotti was not with the other animals. I fed everyone, and was calling to Purcotti to come and eat, but he wasn't home. I went outside and called to him to come eat, but he wasn't there. It wasn't the first time that Purcotti was gone, as he had gone somewhere to visit a girlfriend a couple of times, and he would stay away a day or two and he always came home starving for food! Even though I knew that he was probably visiting, I was still worried about him, because I never knew for certain that he was all right. After breakfast was over, I went out and went for a walk all around the farm, calling to Purcotti, without finding him. I went out to the highway and looked up and down the road to make sure that he had not been hit by a car. I saw no animals on the road at all. I knew that Purcotti loved living on the farm and that he would never leave here for more than a couple of days at a time, so

I tried to quell my worry, and I hoped that he would be home for dinner.

At dinner time all the animals were here for their food except Purcotti. The cats didn't seem to be worried, and the normal cat wrestling was in full swing, though I noticed that it wasn't quite as vigorous as usual, because nobody had to challenge Purcotti. Chays was impatient for her food and was bouncing up and down with intermittent barking. The three cats and Chays all quickly ate their dinner, and then everyone went out for their after-dinner exercise. While we were outside, I called quite a few times to Purcotti with no luck; he didn't show up.

While all the animals were lying around and I watched a ball game, my mind kept wandering, and I thought about Purcotti's disappearance worriedly. I didn't sleep well that night, and I got up in the morning at 6 AM. I went downstairs and out the door, yelling for Purcotti to come home. He still didn't come home so I knew that it was time to go to all the neighbors' houses and ask if anyone had seen him. I fed the animals, and for the first time, they were all subdued, though they all ate well. I think that they were starting to also worry about Purcotti as everyone in the animal family loved him.

I went to every neighbor's house for a couple of miles in each direction, and nobody had seen him. They all promised to call me if he came to their house or if they spotted him at all. It is a horrible feeling to worry about a missing loved one, whether it is a human or an animal, and by this time, I was really worried! I would go out every hour and call him but there was still no success. Since Purcotti had disappeared, I was ignoring a lot of farm work that needed to be done, as I had been fixing fences on the south side of the farm. I decided to go to work, and I petted all the animals, and gave them each a hug, and I went to work.

I got the big Massey Ferguson tractor out of the barn and attached the auger to the back of the tractor so that I could dig fence post holes. I worked for about six hours without a break and realized that it was time to go to the house and feed everyone their evening meal. I drove the tractor back to the barn and parked it, jumping off and yelled for Purcotti. The yell was in vain as he still wasn't home. I had by this time a deep feeling of dread that something terrible had happened to Purcotti. He would never leave the farm for this long! The worry was awful considering I didn't know if he was hurt somewhere or if he might have been killed by a predatory animal. I knew that coyotes were around, but I had not seen one on the farm. The situation was very stressful. I walked to the house and greeted everyone and set to preparing their food for dinner. I looked at the animals who were standing there waiting patiently looking at me. There was no cat wrestling or any frivolity at all. The animal family was worried about Purcotti as much as I was! After everyone ate, we all went outside to walk and do the normal exploring that especially cats will do when they are outdoors. After a couple of hours of being outside, everyone came in and hung out around the house, though the atmosphere was subdued until it was bedtime.

I laid in bed reading a book to deviate my mind from worrying about Purcotti, and one by one, Afja, Marja, Chays, and Sharpie Kitten came up to join me in bed. I thank God it is a big bed, and even with that fact, the animals were laying over different parts of my body! Before I went to sleep, I said a prayer for Purcotti, and I had a tossing, turning, sleepless kind of night.

In the morning nothing was different and looking and calling to Purcotti still didn't bring him home. Days turned into weeks, and with incredible sadness, I had to believe that Purcotti was gone forever. The sad and painful part of losing Purcotti was that life goes on for the living, and the animal family, including me had to go on and find ways to be happy and live our lives.

The new hierarchy of the animal family was structured, and Afja was the new and natural leader. She was an Alpha cat, and the rest of the animal family let her be the matriarch. The play and cat wrestling had resumed, but it was not at the same level of vigor that the family experienced when Purcotti was alive. I noticed that Sharpie Kitten no longer rode Chays, and that he was maturing and being even more vigilant than he was in the past. It was like he knew that the old carefree times were over, and a new reality was upon him after experiencing the pains of life for the first time. He was very wary, and at times jumpy, and he was not the same cat that he used to be when Purcotti was here.

I got up the next morning and made breakfast for the animal family and called everyone to come and eat. Marja and Sharpie Kitten ran downstairs, and Chays came in from outdoors. They were all eating except for Afja; she was not here. I went outside and called to her. She didn't come, so I went to the basement to see if she was there catching a mouse or was into something interesting down there. She wasn't there. I went back outside and called and called but she didn't come. I prayed that she was outside hunting somewhere, as I was starting to compare her disappearance to when Purcotti had disappeared.

I was worried and I couldn't deny that fact as I went to work. I was cutting an oak tree that had fallen down and splitting its wood to be used for winter heating. As I worked, Afja weighed heavily on my mind. I thought to myself that this couldn't be happening again! The horrible part was that it very well could be happening again, and Afja could be gone just like Purcotti. I got done with my work for the day, and as I walked back to the house, I called again and again for Afja. She was not here. I went to the highway, and she wasn't there, and the neighbors hadn't seen her, so I came home to feed the animal family.

Chays was sleeping on the couch and was alone in the house. I went outside and called to Afja, Marja, and Sharpie Kitten. I heard a rustling in the weeds sixty feet from the house, and I again called to the cats. I hoped upon hope that Afja was there, but only Marja and Sharpie Kitten came flying out of the weeds running to the house at full speed! They were on the deck with their fur all standing up and their tails three times fluffier than normal. I said to myself, "Thank God they are okay!" I heard more rustling in the weeds, and I thought, "Could it be Afja?" It wasn't Afja; it was a small female coyote! Everything was completely clear at that point in time. The coyote had killed Purcotti and Afja, and she was after Marja and Sharpie Kitten next!

I don't like killing anything unless I have to, but I realized that I had to defend my animal family, what was left of them. I quickly let Marja and Sharpie Kitten in the house and ran and got my forty-five caliber handgun. I went outside and saw the coyote run past my pickup truck and run into the now dormant garden. The coyote was twenty-five feet away from me as I took aim. The coyote had turned around to look at me and I pulled the trigger. That was one lucky coyote; the gun had jammed! I got it un-jammed, and when the coyote heard the click, she took off running as fast as she could run! I stood there dumbfounded and angry; that rotten coyote had killed Purcotti and Afja, and she had gotten away, at least for now. I figured that since she was after all of the cats, she would be back again. I knew that I had to protect the animal family from any further danger, so I immediately went to the basement dog door, and put plywood over the opening so that the animals could no longer go out on their own. I would have to accompany them when they went out from now on.

When I was finished fixing the door, I came upstairs and fed the animal family. While they were eating, I had a talk with them about what had happened to Purcotti and Afja. Sharpie Kitten seemed to understand, though Marja and Chays just looked at me with a solemn expression. Sharpie Kitten interpreted things to Marja and Chays so they understood. I knew that I could no longer take chances with the animal family's lives, so I traded the forty-five caliber handgun for a Smith and Wesson nine mm automatic handgun that was very reliable. It wouldn't jam if I had to protect the animals. As much as I hated it, I carried the new gun with me for weeks in case the coyote again showed up.

Three weeks later, the coyote did show up. We were all outside for our after-dinner walk and exercise, and the cats were over by the pickup truck. There was a rustle in the bushes and forty feet further away, she was coming out to see if she could kill another of the animal family! I was about thirty-five yards away from her, but I drew my gun, aimed, and fired! The cats were instantly scared and ran for the house as fast as they could run! The shot missed the coyote who was surprised that she was a target. She turned and started to run very fast, and it gave me a straight on target for which to aim. I sighted and fired, hitting the coyote! I was nearly fifty-yards away which is a very lucky hit for a hand weapon, but lucky I was that day. She was killed with one shot. I went to the house to check on the animal family. Marja and Chays were by the door to be let in the house, but I didn't see Sharpie Kitten. I looked under the deck to see if he was hiding, but he wasn't under there. I got up wondering where he had gone, and I heard a familiar "buuurrr rac nakk." ("I'm cool, here I am."). I looked up, and there on the upper deck was Sharpie Kitten. He had climbed up the side of the house again and was safe!

I went to get a shovel to bury the coyote in the woods. While I was working, I reflected on the how the world can be incredibly cruel. The coyote was just trying to feed herself as they are predators of great opportunity, but instead of eating wild animals, she saw easy dinners attacking the animal family. She had to be put away to keep from having all the animals killed, which is still sad. But the moral of the story is, "One must protect their family at all costs."

While all this was transpiring, Sharpie Kitten was angry and very upset. Sharpie Kitten decided to do something positive about the situation instead of being afraid more coyotes would come and kill him. He went up to the computer and started to do research on how not only to kill coyotes, but to rid the farm of coyotes permanently. He saw that fires could work, but that they would also burn down the house, so he rejected that idea. He looked into lightning, but he quickly realized that he couldn't make the lightning go where he wanted it to go or control it at all, so that too was rejected. He looked at animals attacking other animals, and it reminded him of a movie we watched where the Russians stopped the overwhelming number of German tanks from advancing to destroy them in their positions. It was called an "Abatis." The Romans used Abatis to impede their enemies' armies. Trees are felled next to each other, and across each other, and the ends sharpened towards the direction from which an enemy would approach, making their attack impossible, except from a great distance. Sharpie Kitten read many journals from ancient battles to battles during World War II, and he was convinced that this was the way to protect our farm from coyotes.

Sharpie Kitten came running downstairs meowing like crazy after finishing his research. "Merrow, merrrowwww merrowww!" ("Come with me quickly!"). I went to the computer with him, and he showed me the pictures of the Abatis used by the Greeks in the Trojan wars. I looked at Sharpie Kitten, and we both nodded to each other; we would build the Abatis together!

Early the next day, which was a Wednesday, Chays, Sharpie Kitten, and I started work on the project. Marja stayed at home to monitor things from there. With the chainsaw, we felled tree after tree on our western and southern property line. It was the direction from which the coyotes would approach, and it made an impregnable boundary. We worked for five long days, felling and sharpening trees. We were satisfied that coyotes could not enter the farm any longer unless they grew wings and flew over the Abatis in the future!

Even though the Abatis was complete, I still took the animals out for their walks twice a day and stayed with them for protection. The animal family seemed to calm down, and they entered a new time of normalcy on the farm.

Chapter 5

Sharpie Kitten Catches Moles and Fights a Copperhead

A whole year had gone past, and it was now into October. The passing of time had given the animal family time to recover from their family members passing away; and all the animals were relatively happy in their lives. The farm was as productive as always with the last of the garden still producing vegetables with many carrots, onions, peppers, and tomatoes still growing on the plants. The farm was still beautiful, with brilliant maple leaves bright red and gold, and the autumn flowers a vista of dark blue and purple.

The animal family had eaten dinner and we all went out together for our evening walk. As soon as Sharpie Kitten went out the door, he bolted the forty yards to the edge of the yard to the west. He had heard an animal and was on the hunt. His hearing was completely unbelievable, and that he could hear a small animal that far away was an amazing thing to watch. Chays and I walked as silently as we could over to where Sharpie Kitten stood like a statue, staring intently at the bushes six feet away. Marja was thirty yards away standing guard as she was still watching for predators while we all waited for Sharpie Kitten to act. After about ten minutes of standing totally still, he stealthily crawled forward to the edge of the yard bordering berry bushes where he started to rock gently back and forth. He rocked seven times and sprung four feet in the air, pouncing in the bushes. He instantly came back in the yard carrying a very large mole in his mouth! Chays, ever the opportunist, knew another meal was at hand and she followed Sharpie Kitten in hot pursuit. After carrying the mole for over fifty yards he did what cats usually do; that is to drop their prey, to see if it was dead of if he could play

with it as it tried to escape. As soon as he freed the mole, Chays spied her chance and she ran up and grabbed the mole, throwing it in the air, catching it in her mouth and shaking it violently. Chays then did what we knew she would do; she ate the mole in two big bites! Sharpie was standing there with a very satisfied look on his face, as he had a successful hunt, and Chays had an easy snack!

That day Sharpie Kitten had not had enough of hunting and went back to the same spot in the yard to see if more moles would materialize from the bushes, but he didn't have any more luck. In reflection, it was remarkable watching Sharpie Kitten hunt as he either heard the mole, or he could smell it, forty-yards away and he went right to the spot where the mole was hidden. Watching animals act in life is so interesting to observe.

Our routine on the farm had returned to fun and joyous times for the animal family. There was still much play in and outside of the house, with Marja and Sharpie Kitten flying around as fast as possible, chasing each other. They would both mess with Chays and jump on her, but she wasn't as interested in playing with them as she was eating anything that fell on the floor, from any bowl that was unguarded with food in it, or any meal that I was eating. She had a one-track mind, and that track was totally dedicated to food!

Something very different happened on the farm on the last Saturday evening in October.

Chays, Marja, and Sharpie Kitten ran out the door for their after-dinner walk, and they all decided to go north past the garden when suddenly they all stopped dead in their tracks. The fur on their backs and tails stood straight up in the air as they sensed something very dangerous in their midst. I stood thirty feet behind them, and I started scanning the field and surrounding woods for coyotes, bobcats, and bears, but I saw nothing. I looked around for a rock or a big stick to use in case something needed to be driven away from the animals, but I didn't find anything of use there. The hair on the bodies of the animal family was still standing up on their backs and tails, so I knew that something very dangerous was very close by. I decided to run as fast as I could to the house and get my handgun so I could protect the animal family, so off I went. This situation seemed to be dangerous, so I was quick to get there and back.

Sharpie Kitten knew exactly what was there as he had spotted it in the grass at the edge of the field where the woods started. It was a poisonous snake: a copperhead to be exact! The copperhead is a pit viper, very beautiful in its copper color and with hourglass figures from its neck to its tail. The particular snake was a female copperhead getting ready to have her live babies any day. It was three feet long and as large around her body as a very large Polish sausage. When Sharpie Kitten had done his research on how to fight and protect us from predators, coyotes, bobcats, and bears were not the only ones mentioned. The research also mentioned poisonous snakes in the area, which included Rattlesnakes and Copperheads, so Sharpie Kitten in theory at least, knew how to fight poisonous snakes.

Sharpie Kitten could tell something bad was going to happen, as the mother copperhead, when ready to give birth to her live babies, was more territorial than normal, and she was ready to attack the animal family! Sharpie Kitten said, "Meroww blupp brupp." ("Chays, you go ten feet in front of Mrs. Copperhead and keep her attention while Marja and I sneak around behind her."). Chays started jumping around barking loudly, going forward and backward as the snake coiled up, ready to strike at Chays! While Chays was doing her job of keeping the snake's attention, Sharpie Kitten had gone to a maple tree and grabbed a low hanging supple branch and broke it off, pulling backward until it snapped. The branch was about five feet long, and it needed to be split in half, leaving the bottom half of the branch intact and the upper half split, making a fork. When the fork half grabbed the snake, it would hold her in place and she could be moved without any animal getting bitten.

Sharpie Kitten signaled to Marja with his paw and dragged the branch behind Mrs. Copperhead. I had just gotten back to the scene with the gun in my hand, and I saw Sharpie Kitten getting in position to enact their attack on the snake. I aimed my gun at Mrs. Copperhead, but Sharpie Kitten and Marja were so close to her that if I shot, I might hit one of them instead of the snake, so I held my fire, and waited to see what would transpire.

Sharpie Kitten winked at Marja, and he got a strong hold on his end of the branch, while Marja held tightly on her end. They both jumped at the same time grabbing Mrs. Copperhead on the neck right behind her head, pinning her to the ground! Chays was barking furiously at her while her mouth was opening and closing as fast as she could open and close it, trying to bite anything near to her. We could hear her white fangs clicking again and again on her lower teeth as she was desperately trying to escape the forked branch. Sharpie kitten and Marja were holding on as tightly as they could to not injure her but still hold her down until she calmed down enough to move her without getting bitten. After close to five minutes, Mrs. Copperhead calmed down and stopped fighting to get free. I stood there watching incredulously as this took place, and I wondered what Sharpie Kitten was going to do next. Mrs. Copperhead was still very angry, but she was just lying there wondering what would happen to her.

Sharpie Kitten looked at Marja and said, "Mick mick murrruppp" ("Marja, we will drag Mrs. Copperhead to the woods and let go of our stick and run away as fast as we can run!"). Marja and Sharpie Kitten each took a step holding tightly to their ends of the stick, lifting part of the snake and dragging her back end while they walked with her into the woods. As she was being moved, she again became very agitated and angry, opening and closing her mouth, trying to bite and inject her poison in the hated cats! Finally, Sharpie Kitten and Marja had dragged her ten feet into the woods, and they stopped moving. Mrs. Copperhead needed time to calm down again, so that is what the two cats did; waited for five minutes, giving her time to calm down. Sharpie Kitten signaled to Marja that it was time to release their branch and run. Sharpie Kitten meowed to Marja, "Mow burr mow." ("On three we let go."). Sharpie counted to three, and the two cats let go of their branch at precisely the same time and ran like the wind away from Mrs. Copperhead!

After the cats released the branch and Mrs. Copperhead was free, she was still very angry. She was torn between revenge and trying her best to bite Sharpie Kitten, and just being happy that she was alive and free. It was lucky for all involved that she chose to leave and go to her den and give birth to her six baby copperheads three days later!

After Mrs. Copperhead slithered away into the woods, Sharpie Kitten, Marja, and Chays were exhausted, and they returned to the porch deck, and laid happily in the beautiful sunshine. After a while, they all came into the house where I gave them special treats. They all ate and quickly lay down and went soundly to sleep. It was extraordinary to watch the animal family work so well and in a coordinated effort together, defeating another dangerous adversary. Most animals could not have done what these animals just did!

As fall turned into winter, the animal family continued to play, hunt, and have a fun life on the farm. There was a time just after Christmas and the New Year that we got our first big deep snow of the year. Sharpie Kitten couldn't wait to go outside and dive in the snow. Marja didn't want anything to do with the snow, so she stood on her back legs at the door and watched Sharpie Kitten and Chays go outside. I had already shoveled the twenty-five inches of snow off the deck, but I had yet to get the snowblower out and clean the pathways and the yard. Sharpie Kitten moved over the edge of the deck and surveyed the deep snow. He knew if he dove in, he would be over his head in the snow, so he told Chays to go first and make a path for him. "Murrah yehhhrup" ("Chays, you dive in and make a path"). Chays, ever the obedient servant to Sharpie Kitten, dove off the deck into the fresh, fluffy, beautiful snow, and she quickly disappeared from sight! She plowed around under the snow like a doggy submarine, making a tunnel through the yard!

Sharpie Kitten had seen enough; he dove in and came up full of snow. He was transformed into a beautiful white cat with snow crystals all over his body and those incredible emerald green eyes! He saw Chays coming back to the house and decided to make a sneak attack on her as she ran by. Chays ran right next to Sharpie Kitten without seeing him as he was totally buried in the snow when he pounced on her back. Chays was utterly startled, and she ran around in circles in the fresh snow trying to dislodge her rider, still not knowing that it was Sharpie Kitten! Chays yelped and ran for the deck. As soon as she got out of the snow, she knew that she had been the butt of Sharpie Kitten's practical joke and attack, and she spun around quickly, throwing Sharpie Kitten five feet off the deck into the deepest drift, completely covering him with snow! Sharpie Kitten had a snide look on his face as he jumped through the snow back to the deck. He knew for the first time ever Chays had gotten the best of him, and he muttered to himself, "Blurr upp rupp" ("You can't win them all!").

In the country there seems to be routines that go along with living in remote areas, and it was no different for the animal family. Their routine in life was interesting and fun for them even through the cold and snowy winter.

The family watched as time went on, the snow melted, the birds started to sing and return to the farm, and the temperature was rising. You guessed it; spring had arrived, and not only did it signify the usual changing of the seasons, but something was about to happen that brought joy and completely changed the routine of the farm.

Chapter 6

Leo Arrives on the Farm

It was a warm, beautiful day in March with the temperatures in the low sixties here at the farm. A small field mouse ran past the truck with important things to do, and a robin was taking a bath and splashing happily in a large puddle made from the recent rains. The beauty and nature of this place never ceased to amaze me!

It was dinner time, and with the food gobbled down, Sharpie Kitten, Marja, and Chays quickly ran out the door for their evening walk. Sharpie Kitten and Marja went to a bush that was starting to get its green leaves and walked all around it a few times sniffing the air. Chays had run to the pond and was up to her knees in pretty cold water, which didn't seem to bother her at all. Sharpie Kitten watched Chays in the pond and figured that there would be something fun to do there, so he started walking to the pond. Sharpie Kitten was halfway to the water when he stopped completely still in his tracks; there was an intruder present! Marja was watching Sharpie Kitten walk to the pond, and when she saw him stop, she ran for the house as quickly as she could. That was the rule: see an intruder, run to the house! Sharpie Kitten had stood his ground and didn't seem to be afraid, and he was correct in not being afraid as a baby deer, no more than two months old, came walking out of the bushes! It was a male fawn, and he stopped and looked at Sharpie Kitten and Sharpie Kitten looked right back at him, not moving a muscle. Sharpie Kitten knew instantly that the deer would do no harm to the animal family or to himself.

He walked over to the deer and got nose to nose with him, looking into his eyes. The baby deer had very sad, beautiful brown eyes, and after staring at him for a few seconds, Sharpie Kitten said to him, "Marukk meh blulrup?" ("Why do you look so sad?"). The baby deer looked at Sharpie Kitten and said, "Bleh bleh bleahhh!" ("I lost my mom to a hunter, and I'm alone and very hungry!"). I had walked up to Sharpie Kitten and the beautiful baby, (FYI: deer are in the goat family) and realized the baby was very hungry. I didn't have goat feed or goat milk to feed him, so after the animal family was in the house, I drove to town and got plenty of supplies to feed our newest guest.

I arrived back at the farm laden with goodies and I called to the baby deer, "Here little deer," over and over again, but the baby deer was nowhere in sight. I knew that if he didn't eat, he would not survive very long, so I would need to try something else to get him to come back. I went back to the house and called to Sharpie Kitten. I spoke to him in English and a few of his words, but it really didn't matter as he nearly always understood what I was saying to him. I said, "Please come here, Sharpie Kitten!" He came flying down the stairs and then I said to him, "Mewbroww." ("Sharpie Kitten, you have to call the baby deer so he will come back and eat.") He was rubbing against my leg, of course wanting more food, but after I explained things to him, he was ready to go out and help.

I brought out the goat milk and dry food, and Sharpie Kitten and I walked to the pond where the baby deer had come out before. I told him, "Mickyenk." ("Please call him, Sharpie Kitten"). Sharpie Kitten meowed very loudly, "Rouwwww Mouwwww!" ("Come here and eat, you hungry deer!"). We were both looking into the bushes next to us, but he had been hiding in a different bunch of trees and bushes, so we never saw him until the baby deer surprised us both by sneaking up from behind and walking right next to us!

I said to Sharpie Kitten, "Great job!" The baby was standing there looking at us expectantly. I held out the warm bottle of goat milk which he attacked voraciously on his knees! I guess he was used to drinking his mother's milk on his knees, so he continued his routine in that fashion. He wolfed down the entire bottle in less than a minute! I offered him the dry goat food, which he sniffed, but he had no interest in eating. I could see that he wanted to have more milk, so I ran to the house and made another bottle, and then ran back with the warm milk. He saw me coming and ran around in a circle nearly knocking me off my feet to get to the milk! He again got on his knees and drank so hard that he nearly took the bottle out of my hand! He was a very strong animal for being so young.

The baby deer had bonded with us, and we had become his surrogate family just like that! When he had finished his second bottle, he looked at me and bleated, "Bleahhh." ("Thank You!"). He still didn't want the dry food, and after again sniffing the food, walked to the pond, and went right in the fairly cold water! He didn't stay in the water long, as he jumped high in the air and ran out of the water and into the nearby woods. I was thinking to myself, "This is so neat!" I knew that taking care of the baby deer was going to be a long process, but I've always felt that we were supposed to help all of God's creatures, so I was ready to do whatever was necessary to raise the little deer. Sharpie Kitten had watched the baby run into the woods, and he thought to himself, "Burrrruppup!" ("This is so neat!").

Sharpie Kitten and I walked back to the house and while we walked, I thought it was a good time to give the baby deer a name. He needed an identity, especially if he was going to be part of our animal family. I got Sharpie Kitten, Marja, and Chays together, and asked them what they thought would be a good name for the baby deer. Chays at first didn't care what we called him, but after she went to her bowl and started chewing on her pork bone, she stopped chewing, and looked up at us. She barked, "Raa ufff!" ("Call him, 'Hambone!'") Marja and Sharpie Kitten and I all looked at each other, and shook our heads. Chays didn't care anymore as she had her ever-consuming meat! Marja said in her high voice, "Mick, mick, mick, mick" (It meant, "Mickey Mantle," who was her favorite baseball player in the history of baseball). Sharpie Kitten still was not happy with those name choices. Marja and I both looked at Sharpie Kitten and waited for his answer. Chays was up to her neck in pork bone and didn't care if the world came to an end! Sharpie Kitten had been on the computer yesterday doing research on infections in the claws of cats from fighting, and had come across lions in Africa, who had gotten the greatest percentage of infections because of the intense heat. There was one lion in particular who was educating many of the lions there on how to obtain antibiotics to stem their infections, and his name was Leo. He was one of the leaders of the largest pack of lions, and was not only fierce and strong, but he was very smart. Sharpie Kitten knew that the baby had to be smart, strong, fierce, and very fast just so that he could survive the hunters who would love to make a meal out of him. He also needed those attributes to manage the icy cold winters, where food was scarce. Sharpie Kitten looked up at me and said, "Rowoo Rahupp." ("Let's call him 'Leo'"). I looked at Marja and back at Sharpie Kitten and I told them both, "It is official. He is now named 'Leo!'"

I got up early the next morning, and with the bottle filled with warm goat milk and a container with dry goat mix, Sharpie Kitten and I headed for the pond. Sharpie Kitten didn't complain that I was feeding Leo before he got his breakfast because he realized that the baby was very vulnerable, and his needs were greater than his own needs. When we arrived, I yelled, "Leo, Leo, come get your breakfast!" Leo didn't appear. He probably doesn't know we are calling to him as he has never heard his new name. I looked at Sharpie Kitten, and he looked back at me with his beautiful sparkling green eyes, and he called to Leo, "Roww brak Raa oww!" ("Heh Leo, come and eat your breakfast!"). Leo instantly appeared like magic! Sharpie Kitten and his abilities were really something special!

Sharpie quickly ran and climbed a tree to keep from being stepped on by Leo in his frenzy to eat. Leo again got down on his knees to suck the nipple on the bottle, simulating feeding from his mom. He drank the entire bottle in thirty seconds, so I went back to the house to make another bottle. Sharpie Kitten had stayed in his tree, as he decided for now that was a safe place to be, especially when Leo was so hungry that he didn't notice anything going on around him except his food! I came back and Leo ran for me, wagging his tail rapidly back and forth, which he continued to do while drinking his second bottle. I guess the tail wagging was something baby deer did while preparing to and actually eating their food. He sucked the bottle furiously and butted his head against the bottle and my hand while he drank, which was also something he had done with his momma. He was drinking the bottle so hard and fast that I had to hold the bottle with both hands to keep him from taking it away from me!

When Leo had finished his second bottle, I decided to get him to try his dry goat feed. Sharpie Kitten saw that it was finally safe to come down from the tree, so when he was on the ground, he came over to us and showed Leo that the dry food was good by acting like he had taken a bite. Leo watched him closely, and followed suit with Sharpie Kitten and took a bite of his dry food. He got a large bite of the food and started to blow bits of the food out of his mouth all over the place, making a "Pruuuup, pruuup, pruuup" noise. He was eating and spitting food, spraying it all over Sharpie Kitten who ran back and again climbed his tree to escape the barrage! With Sharpie Kitten out of the way, I became his proud recipient, and I caught a big glob of food on my neck! He finally got the hang of eating the dry goat food, and was eating in a much slower, cleaner manner before he finished. Leo had a full belly, so he went back to the woods for a nap.

As days on the farm went by, we watched Leo grow right before our eyes.

He was now drinking three bottles of goat milk at a time, and then eating his dry food for dessert. I saved time and trips to the house by bringing a bucket of warm milk out to continue filling Leo's bottle as he drank. He was incredibly impatient while waiting for me to refill the bottle and he would nearly knock me over while I was filling it. Leo was still furiously wagging his tail and he bleated in a high voice, "Blehh bleeehhhh" ("Great milk!").

Sharpie Kitten always analyzed everything that was going on and tried to do things the easy way. He figured that we shouldn't have to go to the pond to feed Leo. He said, "Bbbrick na mow." ("I'll call Leo to come here to the house to eat."). I thought that Sharpie Kitten's idea was great, and I told him so, "Braarrup!" ("That is a great idea, Sharpie Kitten!"). I was getting better and better at speaking to Sharpie Kitten in his own "Catenese" language.

The animal family had eaten and had come outside for their evening walk, so we decided to give Sharpie Kitten's idea the real trial. I got the pail of milk ready with one bottle filled and I yelled for Leo, "Leo come and eat your dinner." Leo didn't come out. I yelled again, "Leooooo, come and eat!" I saw him come out over by the pond, but he didn't make a move to come to the house. I looked at Sharpie Kitten who already knew what needed to be done. He called to Leo in a very loud voice, "Brickkk na mowww!" ("Come over here Leo and eat your dinner!"). Leo instantly looked up, bleated happily, "Blahh blehh" ("Oh boy, food!") and came running over to us jumping up on the deck in his excitement. The animal family scattered to keep from getting trampled with Marja running under the table, Chays going behind me, and Sharpie Kitten doing his normal escape routine, climbing up the corner of the house to jump the ten feet from his perch to the upper deck. He walked over to the edge of the deck and put his head through the rails, watching Leo who had begun to eat. Sharpie Kitten always understood the important things in life, and his skills speaking with animals of different species were phenomenal!

Weeks and months passed peacefully on the farm, and the time found Leo growing like a weed. He had lost nearly all of his fawn camouflage spots that baby deer are born with, and we could see how formidable he would become later as a big buck in the local deer community. He came to the house every day to eat without being called, and he now only ate dry goat feed and corn, as his milk days were long over.

Leo walked every evening with the animal family all over the farm, looking at and eating different plants, nibbling tender leaves that he liked best. Chays decided to try a leaf and she chewed it for a second, spitting it out! She mumbled "Bruff ruff" ("I wonder why I did that, I'm not a goat!").

Sharpie Kitten took it upon himself to be a mentor to Leo, just like Purcotti had mentored him as a kitten. Sharpie Kitten was teaching Leo not just the fun things in life but things that were important in his future. He talked about dangers that existed for Leo, especially about the hated coyotes, and how Leo could be hurt or killed by them. Leo got very scared when he heard this story, so Sharpie Kitten told Leo about the Abatis, and how most of the farm was protected by its presence. He also told Leo that if he stayed in this part of the farm, he would be relatively safe. Leo didn't know that there was a different kind of world out there that would give him great pleasure along with ultimate danger to his life.

Male deer after maturity usually travel quite a few miles in a large circle to feed and find mates to breed, and of course, fight each other during rutting season. This fighting occurs so that the strongest male deer, or as they are known as "Bucks," will make the deer herd as strong and tough as possible for survival. Leo was still very young so he didn't understand any of this stuff yet, but his time would come. Sharpie Kitten explained to Leo about the most dangerous thing he would encounter in his life: hunters and how they would be happy to kill him and make food out of him! This last statement really scared Leo! He tried to calm Leo down so he also explained how to hide from hunters so he would be safe.

There was something else that Leo didn't understand, and that was that he was a deer! Leo couldn't grasp the concept that he was different from Sharpie Kitten, Marja, and Chays, and though Sharpie Kitten was exceptionally intelligent, he had yet to figure out how to show Leo that there were so many different kinds of animals on earth.

A week later a couple of good friends of mine, Nina and Meghan, were coming to visit with their young daughters, Bryn and Rosie. I had told them about Leo, and they all wanted to meet him. They had been here many times and they always enjoyed the beauty and peaceful surroundings of the farm.

Early on the morning of my friends' arrival, Sharpie Kitten ran to the door, and stood on his back legs, with his front paws on the glass of the storm door. He was intently looking outside. Leo had not yet had his breakfast of corn and goat food, so I picked up the container and filled it as I figured that Leo was at the door. He was at the door, and I watched as the door magically opened! Leo had gotten his head against the door handle pushing the black button, and when the mechanism clicked, he put his nose in the door and popped it open. There was only one thing that could possibly happen at this point, and that was Leo walking happily into the house! Sharpie Kitten had stepped aside to let Leo walk by. He stopped and stared at the morning news on TV. He had never seen a TV before and was totally fascinated by it. I walked over to Leo, petted him, and told him we should go outside so that he could have his breakfast. He saw the food container in my hand, and joyfully and hungrily followed me back outside to eat. His food was much more important to him than watching TV!

After Leo had eaten his breakfast, I figured that the excitement was over until noon when Meghan and Nina would arrive with their children, but I was wrong. Sharpie Kitten was again standing on his back legs looking out the door, wanting desperately to go outside. He was scratching at the door, and said, "eeh oou" ("Let me out quickly!"). I looked out and I didn't see any danger, so I let him go outside. Sharpie Kitten took off as fast as he could run, straight for the garden. I was thinking to myself, "What could possibly be going on now?" It didn't take long to find out what was going on as there was Leo in the carrot patch, pulling up carrots! He pulled one out of the ground, threw it in the air then caught it in his mouth eating the green end first, then devouring the sweet carrot! I watched transfixed until he had eaten his third carrot. I yelled at him to stop, and he instinctively jumped back. I clapped my hands together so Leo would leave the garden and go eat leaves elsewhere. I knew that I would have to pick carrots or Leo would come back and eat all of them! He took off running in quick circles and making moves like an all-pro wide receiver in the NFL! Then he ran around the barn and disappeared from sight. I thanked Sharpie Kitten for saving the carrot patch, because without him, I would not have known Leo the destroyer was at work!

Sharpie Kitten and I walked back to the house and prepared to meet our guests in a couple of hours.

Our friends arrived on schedule, and we all hugged and said our greetings. Nina and Meghan are both nurse practitioners, and they are great ladies with huge hearts. They are both blonds, look a lot like sisters, and they are super moms and wives to their children and husbands. It is wonderful to have them as friends.

We ate outside and had a fun lunch with animated conversation. The food consisted of homemade taco salad and freshly made salsa with all of the ingredients straight from the garden, except for On The Border chips. An ice-cold Dos Equis beer went along beautifully with the Mexican food.

With our lunch completed and dishes cleaned up, I told everyone that

I would call Leo so that they could meet him. We especially wanted their daughters to meet Leo and interact with him. Meghan's daughter Bryn was five years old, and already a lover of all living things whether it is a butterfly, a bird, or a snake! She has a family dog which she loves, her own miniature horse, and some rabbits. She is a darling child with such a love for animals that I predict she will become a great veterinarian someday. Rosie, who is only a year old, also shows many signs of being an animal lover, as she also plays with her families' long-haired dachshunds.

I got a container of corn so that Bryn could feed Leo when he came, and I got everyone outside in the yard in anticipation of his arrival. I yelled his name loudly, "Leo, Leo, come and visit and eat." We looked around, but Leo hadn't come. I waited a minute and called him again, with no better result than the first time I called. Leo had only met a couple of my friends in the six months he had been living happily on the farm, so I thought that he might have been reticent to come out. I called him a couple of more times and he still didn't appear. I knew though that I had the secret weapon; I called Sharpie Kitten to help! Sharpie Kitten was stretched out, languishing in the sun's warmth and watching the show in the yard from the upper deck. I asked him, "Sharpie Kitten, please call Leo." He gave me a look like, "Gee, is that all?" He meowed loudly, "Brrrurrr ak now!" ("Heh Leo, some people want to meet you, so come on out!") About a minute later, Leo appeared in the yard, and he stopped walking ten feet away from the children. Nina and Meghan had their cameras out as they didn't want to miss this great and rare encounter of their children with this wonderful young deer. The beautiful children stood stock still so as not to scare Leo, and to see what he was going to do. I slowly walked out in the yard and gave the container of corn to Bryn and called to Leo to come and eat. Leo's ears perked up as he saw a meal in front of him which was something that he always attacked with glee;

whomever held the container of food was a friend of his! He walked slowly over to the girls, but before he went to Bryn to eat, he totally stopped in front of Rosie and looked at her. Rosie raised her arms up high, and Leo came to her and kissed her on the nose! Rosie laughed happily, as Leo then walked to Bryn who held out the container in her hand and began devouring the corn. Bryn petted Leo soothingly while he ate his lunch. Leo was always a voracious eater, and he didn't disappoint anyone or deviate from the norm and ate every last kernel of corn in the container. When he finished his meal, he brushed his head against Bryn gently and calmly walked over to the bushes and nibbled at his favorite leaves. We all stood and watched him eat until he walked into Purcotti's Jungle and disappeared from sight.

Soon after Leo left, my friends and I said our goodbye's as they had long drives ahead of them to go back to their families. All in all, it had been a magical day!

Time was passing and I could tell that Leo was becoming restless. He would go and stay in the woods for a day or two, without coming for food. I don't think he really knew what he was doing or why that he was doing it but watching him grow up was an interesting and worrisome process. One day a couple of female deer showed up and Leo looked at them without moving. Finally, he walked to them and the three of them sniffed each other. Leo didn't make a definitive move and the females lost interest and walked away from him.

Sharpie Kitten watched that encounter and knew that he had to make Leo understand that he was a deer and not a cat, and that Leo needed to spend time with his own species. Sharpie Kitten, after eating his favorite brain food which consisted of salmon, lobster, clams, and shrimp scampi snacks, thought about the situation. He formulated a plan to educate and help Leo make a giant step in his life.

After dinner, Sharpie Kitten, Marja, and Chays went on their walk, and Sharpie Kitten called to Leo to come and join them, "Braaaa ou!" ("Heh Leo, come and hang out with us!") Leo came out of the woods, and after he and Sharpie Kitten touched noses in greeting, he started his conversation with Leo. He told Leo that he really needed to understand that the reason that he was spending more and more time away in the woods, was because that was what deer do normally in life: "Mac merr ou brrruu nya." Leo stood there not understanding what Sharpie Kitten was trying to tell him. Leo had spent nearly all of his life here on the farm with Sharpie Kitten, Marja, and Chays, and he just didn't realize that he was a different species from the animal family. Sharpie Kitten said to Leo, "Yurrann bluurrp ma mouu." ("Leo, please come with me.").

Sharpie Kitten led Leo over to the garden where a two-foot tall water tank was situated, and which was used to water the plants and for animals to be able to have a drink when they were thirsty. Sharpie Kitten got on his hind legs and put his front paws on the edge of the water tank, with his head over the edge so that he could see the water. Leo walked over to the tank next to his friend and he looked over the edge at the water. Leo saw his reflection for the first time! Sharpie Kitten's black head and sparkling green eyes shone back at him, and he saw his own beautiful brown eyes and deer head, reflecting back at him. Leo stood and stared, and the light went on in his mind, and he finally knew the truth. Sharpie Kitten was a large, beautiful black cat, and he was a handsome deer! He walked to Sharpie Kitten and kissed his nose and rubbed his nose against Sharpie Kitten's silky black fur. After looking deeply into Sharpie Kitten's emerald green eyes, Leo turned and without looking back, walked through the field into the thick woods.

Leo was gone for a week before he came to the house to have a container of corn and to say hello to everyone. He turned after eating and walked right back into the woods. Leo was now spending all his time with the deer that lived here on the farm, and we didn't see him again until springtime.

Leo showed up at the house on a beautiful warm early spring day to visit us for a short period of time, complete with his new antlers. It was interesting about his antlers, as normally a one-year-old deer has spike antlers, thus the name, spike buck. Leo, who had an enormous amount of nutritious proteins and grains his first year on earth broke the normal rule and had two points on each side of his antlers. His antlers looked like a deer that was two years old instead of one year old. Leo was here long enough to say hi and of course, eat some corn! When he finished his meal, he once again walked away into the woods with Chays, Marja, and Sharpie Kitten sitting in the sun watching him stroll away.

Epilogue

The animal family continues to thrive and completely enjoy life here on the farm, complete with their funny antics that make them so lovable. Sharpie Kitten, Marja, Chays, and I all want to thank you for spending time with us, and we send our love and joy to all who read or listen to this story.

There will be more stories and updates from us in the future, including the possibility of Sharpie Kitten running for political office. He has a plan that will unite both parties and especially unite our country, so please stay tuned for that!

The End

Bryn feeds Leo some corn while Rosie watches closely.

Chays happily guarding Sharpie Kitten.

Chays takes Leo on patrol.

Leo in the wild at two years old.

Leo kisses Rosie as Bryn looks on.

Leo kissing Sharpie Kitten.

Leo taking his daily bath.

Marja and Afja happy together.

Marja and Leo kiss hello.

Marja coming to join the fun.

Purcotti and Sharpie Kitten relax after workout.

Purcotti teaching Sharpie Kitten to Fight.

Sharpie Kitten at two years old.

Sharpie Kitten in his tree watching Leo eat.

Sharpie Kitten whispers to Leo.

Sharpie Kitten, Marja, Chays, and Leo.

Sharpie Kitten's race partner Johann and his mom Doerniece.

The Black Kitten is home.